Let's Learn Aesop's Fables

The Lion and the Mouse

WINDMILL BOOKS

Published in 2018 by Windmill Books, an Imprint of Rosen Publishing | 29 East 21st Street, New York, NY 10010

CATALOGING-IN-PUBLICATION DATA
Title: The lion and the mouse.
Description: New York : Windmill Books, 2018. | Series: Let's learn Aesop's fables
Identifiers: ISBN 9781499483741 (pbk.) | ISBN 9781499483697 (library bound) | ISBN 9781499483598 (6 pack)
Subjects: LCSH: Fables. | Folklore.
Classification: LCC PZ8.2.A254 Li 2018 | DDC 398.2--dc23

Manufactured in China.
CPSIA Compliance Information: Batch BS17WM: For Further Information contact Rosen Publishing, New York, New York at 1-800-237-9932

There was once a great lion who lived on the grassy plains close to the edge of the jungle. Each day he roamed the grasslands, checking that all was well in his kingdom.

He feared no one,
but everyone
feared him.

The zebra mothers warned their babies about the lion.

"Stay away from the lion. Keep your distance and all will be well."

And the elephant mothers warned their babies too.

"I am far too big for the lion to hunt, but you are small. Stay close to me and all will be well."

When it grew too hot
during the day, the lion
would walk into the jungle
where it was cool and dark
in the shade of the trees.

He would roam
through the shady
jungle until he
reached his cave.

There he slept for
a few hours each day.

A family of mice

also lived in the jungle. They had a nest in a hole in a tree, and each day the young mice were sent to look for food.

One of the little mice was
particularly curious,
and he often ventured further
than his brothers and sisters.

One day, the mouse reached the edge of the jungle. He saw the great plains of grass and herds of animals.

He gasped in fear at the sight of the mighty lion on his rock and scurried back into the jungle.

Each day, the little
mouse saw the lion
walking to his cave to
sleep, and his curiosity
got the better of him.

He just had
to look inside
the cave.

So one day, the mouse decided to visit the lion's cave. He knew the lion was on the plains, so he crept through the jungle until he arrived at the mouth of the cave.

Dare he go any further?

"ROAAAAR!"

A giant paw trapped the mouse. It was the lion! "Please let me go!" begged the mouse. "I wasn't causing trouble!"

13

"Well you ARE in trouble!" growled the lion. "What are you doing in my cave?"

"Just being curious, Sir! But if you let me go, I promise one day I will do you a favor."

14

The lion laughed. "As if you could help me, king of the beasts! You are so small, but you seem quite brave. Be gone — and NEVER come back here again!"

The mouse scampered away.

Some weeks later,
as he prowled through
the jungle, the lion walked
into a trap. A big net of
ropes fell on top of him.

The more he struggled to free himself, the more entangled he became. He realized the hunter would return soon.

Exhausted, he lay still and roared softly.

Then the lion saw a tiny creature standing in front of him. It was the mouse.

"Let me help you," squeaked the mouse, and he set to work gnawing the ropes.

Before long, the ropes fell away from the lion and he gave a mighty shake. The mouse found himself scooped up in a giant paw.

"Thank you," growled the lion.

Suddenly the lion placed the mouse on his back. "Hold on tight to my mane," he instructed.

And then they were racing through the jungle. The mouse held on tightly and squeezed his eyes shut.

The lion arrived at the grassy plain and gave a mighty ROAR!

The animals looked up in fear.

"Meet my friend the mouse," said the lion. "He helped me escape the hunter's trap. The small really can help the strong."

And from that day on,
the lion and the mouse
were best friends.

Little friends may prove
to be great friends.